The Godde

Graeme Hall

First published August 2020 by Fly on the Wall Press

Published in the UK by

Fly on the Wall Press

56 High Lea Rd

New Mills

Derbyshire

SK22 3DP

www.flyonthewallpoetry.co.uk

ISBN: 978-1-913211-25-7

Typesetting and Cover Design by Isabelle Kenyon.

Cover Image public domain work: "Een schip op volle zee" (Dutch name as stated by the Rijksmuseum). The scene depicts the goddess Mazu and the Song embassy to Goryeo of 1123 on the high seas. Mazu is dressed in red, holds a hu tablet, and hovers on a cloud above one of the ship's masts. A high official, presumably Lu Yundi, is likewise dressed in red and is shown kneeling in prayer. The clothing is in the style of the Song dynasty.

A CIP Catalogue record for this book is available from the British Library.

Supported using public funding by

ARTS COUNCIL
ENGLAND

LOTTERY FUNDED

For Anne

CONTENTS

A Short History of Chinese Tea

Today I am meeting my husband for the first time. He is in the drawing room talking with my mother and I can hear their muffled voices as I prepare tea. I watch as the pearls unfold in the water and a fragment of jasmine petal drifts amongst the unravelling leaves. From a neighbouring house, a radio is playing a recent hit and I sing along quietly.

I enjoy making tea, a skill I learnt from my aunt, and I take pleasure in the attention to detail that is needed. I know, for example, that for jasmine the water should not be too hot, but instead should have crab eyes. It was my aunt who taught me how to judge the temperature of boiling water from the size of the bubbles. Shrimp eyes the coolest, and then crab eyes, fish eyes, rope of pearls and raging torrent. I smile at the memory, wishing my aunt was here to help me today.

I concentrate on the tea to try and overcome my nerves. I know how important this day is and I didn't need to be told to use our finest teapot. According to family tradition, it was given as a gift by a Court official who had been stranded in our village in bad weather. Like all the best, it is made of Yixing clay, a lustrous, reddish-brown with no frivolous decoration or ornament, just fine calligraphy. Sitting on top of the lid is a delicately-crafted turtle. The teapot is one of the few precious items that came with us when we fled to Macau after the war.

Mother told me last week that a marriage had been arranged. I wasn't surprised; I'd had my suspicions for some time. Hushed conversations partly overheard behind closed doors. I don't mind. I know I could refuse if I wanted to, but I won't, unless he turns out to be completely hideous. I know what's expected of me. I don't think I am vain, but I am lucky that my looks will help get the good match that's needed to restore the family to prosperity. Lam Fung - that's his name - is the son of a wealthy businessman. I just pray that he's acceptable.

When the tea is ready, I place everything on a tray and carry it into the room next door. I try hard not to look directly at him and keep my head bowed as I place the tray on the rosewood side table. I turn to leave the room but my mother asks me to stay.

"Lei-Wai, please sit down." I do as she asks and take the chair next to her. I keep my head bowed but I cannot resist looking aside to see the man I will spend the rest of my life with. I catch a glimpse of fine features and I feel overwhelming relief. "Lei-Wai," continues my mother, "this is Lam Fung." I take my mother's cue to look at him properly and my initial impression is confirmed. He is a handsome man.

I am a little tongue-tied. What do you say when introduced to your future husband? "It is a pleasure to meet you," is all I can manage.

"The pleasure is all mine." He is gracious in response.

I pour the tea and we make polite conversation: the weather is poor for the time of year, but business is good. We discuss mutual acquaintances and the latest films from Hong Kong. I am becoming more at ease with the situation when my mother brings the conversation to an end.

"Lei-Wai, I have matters to discuss with our guest. Would you please take the tea things away?"

As I get up, he also stands and that's when I see the darkness in his eyes. I feel uneasy and I try not to look. Try not to stare. Try not to say anything at all.

*

My mother brings me tea and places it by the side of my bed. She pours a cup and I lever myself up until I am partly sitting. Oolong. The tea has been well-prepared and it's a good choice. I know that it will help me recover.

He has only been to see me once since it happened. Even then, he could barely look at me. It was as if I had let him down. As if I had betrayed him. Mother tells me that he is just upset. She says he will come round in time. That we can try again. I'd like to believe her but I don't know. She is trying to reassure me, but I have an uneasy feeling that nothing will be the same. In the meantime, though, all I want to do is sleep. I am so tired that I don't even dream. I prefer it that way.

I wake when the maid knocks on the door. She collects the tea things before leaving silently. She doesn't want to talk to me either. I've never trusted the girl and more than once I've seen the way he looks at her. He thinks I don't notice but I'm not blind.

The bruises are healing, at least. I guess I was lucky that I didn't break anything. How did it happen anyway? As I slowly recover my strength, I've been trying to remember, but it is coming back only hazily. The only thing I know for certain is that I found myself lying at the bottom of the stairs. A sharp pain gripped my belly and a line of blood ran down the inside of my left thigh.

The maid is back with soup. She has a cold look that is at odds with her seventeen years. I wish we'd never taken her in. I was too sentimental and fell for a sob story about her parents. She's useless at her job and I've often said that we should get someone else, but he always speaks up for her. She's young, he says, give her a chance. Oh, she's young alright, I'm well aware of that.

Lying in bed, there is little to do but listen to the noise of the street. The area is quiet but there are still the hawkers who shout out their wares. I hear sounds in the house as well. Doors opening and closing, comings and goings. I hear voices too. Sometimes I think I hear the two of them talking and I strain to make out words. My imagination fills in where my ears fail me.

They say I must have slipped on the stairs but I have no memory of how or why. I wasn't carrying anything and there was nothing on them to make the steps slippery. How could I have fallen?

Mother comes every day and makes tea. I'm touched, as I know that the tea she has brought is expensive. It has good health-giving properties and I can feel my strength slowly returning. As my body starts to recover, my memory is slowly filling in some of the gaps. I remember that I was on the landing talking to the maid. No, not talking, *remonstrating* about something…about what I'm not sure…when she brushes past me, knocking me off-balance…

*

The tea gives me the strength I need. Pu'er has a dark maturity that matches my mood these days. My husband, on the other hand, prefers alcohol. In the past, it was just rice wine after a banquet, or a European wine if he was trying to impress buyers from Hong Kong. I don't know when it was that he started with whisky, but now it seems to be all he drinks.

I tried hiding the bottles at first, but he soon put a stop to that with his fist. Trying to be more subtle, I took to pouring whisky down the drain when he was out. Not to empty the whole bottle - he'd be suspicious of that - but to try and reduce the amount he drank. It didn't work. He didn't say anything, but pretty soon he started locking the bottles away in his study.

I don't go out much these days. He doesn't like me to and unless I can shield my face, I don't want to either. I wish my mother were still alive. She'd know what to do.

He's never forgiven me for not giving him a child. It doesn't seem to occur to him that I also felt the loss. The doctors said that the internal injuries were probably too bad, but also, he stopped sleeping with me so I don't know how he thought it could happen anyway. It's been years since we shared a bed. He takes his pleasures elsewhere, of course, but at least to begin with he had the decency to be discreet about it. Now he seems to enjoy making sure that I know who he's seeing. Once, when I was laid up in bed with flu, he even brought someone home. I think he did that on purpose. Perhaps it gave him a thrill. Sometimes I think I should never have kicked out the maid; at least then I could have kept the shame within the house. I made sure that every maid we had after her was older than me. Something else he has never forgiven me for.

The tea is dark and earthy. There is a complexity in the taste that I would never have enjoyed when I was young.

*

Perhaps I was always destined to have this tea-shop, even if it took a long time to get here. The irony is that I probably wouldn't have it if it hadn't been for his drinking. It was liver failure apparently. I can't exactly say I was sad, even if there was a small part of me that wondered what might have been. If things had turned out the way my younger self thought they would. Of course, even at the end he had one final joke at my expense. Where I thought that there would be money to live comfortably, instead there were debts. When everything was finished, there was just enough left to buy the tea-shop.

A love of tea seems to run in the family and I remember the lessons that my aunt taught me. I have found my vocation at last and I get to drink all sorts of different teas: creamy White Peony, delicate Silver Needle, fresh Dragon Well. I still drink simple jasmine and I don't mind being reminded of my naïve younger self. I've forgiven her now, but as I get older, I return more and more to Oolong, in a bid to keep both my cholesterol and blood pressure low. So much more pleasurable than the pills the doctor gives me.

And what am I drinking today? Nanjing Rainflower tea. It comes from the hills around our ancestral village and I can't drink it without thinking of my aunt. I make sure that I prepare it properly. Shrimp eyes, always shrimp eyes, she tells me.

And All Will Be Well

The old men say she is often seen at half-light; sometimes at dawn, more often dusk. Occasionally she appears when there's a mist, or when low clouds descend and Taipa and Coloane are obscured. When light is shaded, when Macau is in a transitory condition balanced between existence and non-existence, that is when it is possible to see a young woman in a red dress, looking out to sea. Some people are doubtful and ask why it is that she is never seen in broad daylight, why it is that she seems to be seen more often when sailors have been enjoying the camaraderie of a bar. The fishermen and seafarers dismiss such talk as the idle nonsense of land folk who know nothing of her ways. They know that she is always with them, and when she is with them, all is well.

The men are tired. They have barely finished sluicing down the deck after their last sailing and the smell of fish hangs around them. They've had a good catch – a large enough haul of snapper and coral trout that, as far as everyone except the skipper is concerned, means there's no need to go out again for a few days. What they want is time at home with their wives and families, or at least time in the bars and backstreet gambling dens playing dice and losing what hasn't already been spent on beer and women. But the skipper is having none of that.

"No slacking, come on guys. One more big one, that's what we want, just one more and then we can take a break."

They hate him for saying it, but it's true. The fish are there in numbers. It's obvious. Last time out, no sooner had they dropped the net, when they felt the weight of the catch. It was a struggle to haul it in.

"Come on, the fish won't wait for us," he continues. "Let's get this finished, then a few hours kip and we'll go again."

There are four of them in total: the skipper, two of his cousins, and Ling-wah, the youngest at nineteen. The skipper of the somewhat ramshackle fishing junk is a man in his forties, even if he looks older than that, his youth surrendered to the wind, sun and rain. He is Tanka born and bred. He no longer keeps chickens on board the way his parents and grandparents did, but the hen coops are still there and sometimes he looks at them longingly. His wife used to look after the birds and normally she would still be one of the crew, but she is eight months gone with their second child and although she hates being away from the water, she is land-bound these days. Ling-wah has been with them for the last two years. He is the only one of the four who isn't Tanka, which means he is often the butt of jokes based on his lack of sea-faring experience. Yet he has always been drawn to the sea, known since he was a small boy that the sea was where he belonged, though getting on board had been a battle of wills on all sides. His parents had objected from the start, they'd even managed to get him a job as a kitchen boy at the *Santa Casa di Misericordia*, which hadn't worked out, but eventually they gave in. The skipper and his crew were equally unenthusiastic – they'd never sailed before with someone who wasn't Tanka – but the skipper's wife had had the final word. "*There's something about him,*" she told her husband. "*I think he'll bring us luck.*"

*

He was six the first time he saw her. He'd been playing at the water's edge, looking for treasures washed up from passing tramp steamers on the way to Guangzhou and the ports upriver. The sun was starting to go down and it was time for home; his mother would be cross if he was late again. The woman was standing barefoot on a rock that jutted out from the sea-wall and he was puzzled as to how she had got there. The wall was high at that point and the rock she was standing on a distance below, but it was the dress that caught his eye as much as anything — a vivid red that shone as the daylight began to ebb away. A colour of celebration and special occasions, the red of weddings and *lai see* packets, and she stood out in a city recovering from the hardships of war. Two days later, he was at the same spot but she was not to be seen, and with the quicksilver consciousness of a child, his attention was soon devoted to the ephemera of the shoreline and she disappeared from his thoughts.

*

A decision is made.

"We're going to the Nine Islands," the skipper says. "They say the *shek baan yu* are there in numbers. You can hear them from Black Sand beach, croaking and grunting the way they do."

"You're kidding, right?" Cousin No. 1, a skinny man with muscles like tightly-coiled fishing lines, but also with a slight limp from favouring his left leg. The consequence of an accident some years back.

"What's wrong with going back to Taipa?" This from Cousin No. 2, the inverse of Cousin No. 1, a large man with a high-maintenance stomach.

The skipper is insistent. "Everybody's at Taipa these days."

"Yeah well, there's a reason for that," says Cousin No. 2, who isn't giving up without a fight.

Kau Chau. The Nine Islands. Chinese islands in Chinese waters. They've long been favoured fishing grounds and nobody has worried about who owned them. But things are different now. There are patrol boats with loudhailers and Party slogans, and — more to the point —

guns and Red Guards happy to use them. The Portuguese police aren't much better: tense, always on the lookout for refugees, and just as trigger-happy as their Red counterparts. Five bodies were found the week before, washed up in the coastal mangrove swamps. Nobody asks Ling-wah's opinion, not that it would make a difference. If the skipper says they are going to the Nine Islands, then that's where they're going.

*

A few weeks later the boy saw the woman again. This time she was standing on a disused finger pier, up at Fai Chi Kei in the Inner Harbour. The wooden struts that supported the pier were rotting away and several of the planks that made up the walkway were missing, and those that remained looked as if a foot might go through them easily. He could see that one of them was about to give way and even at his age, it looked a dangerous place to stand.

'Hello?!' he called out. No response. He tried again, but if she'd heard him, then she was paying no attention. A padlocked gate stopped him from getting closer, but he was sure that he had to do something, even if he didn't know what, so he ran home, sprinting down dark, moss-covered alleys and *travessas*, to the house that his family shared with two others. His mother was preparing food. He told her about the strange woman out on that old pier by the docks.

'She might fall in, come and see!'

His mother told him to be quiet, to help set the table.

'But *Mah-ma*!'

'Quiet now!' the firm reply.

Later, after supper, the boy crept out of the house and returned to the pier. It was dark, but there was enough streetlight to see that there was no sign of her. She must be dead. The only conclusion. Washed out into the sea. There was no other explanation for why she was not there when he went back. He did not consider the simple possibility that she had left her precarious position. He assumed the worst. She had been in danger, anyone could see that, and when he had returned she was no longer there. The splintered planks that had fallen into the waters had not been there before, of that he was sure. There was only one explanation, the logic incontestable, and yet for all that, he was not particularly surprised when he saw her several weeks later, this time standing at the prow of a *lorcha* as it moved out of the harbour into the fairway, heading for open waters.

She must live on that boat, he said to himself, though even at his young age he recognised that he had never seen a boatwoman wearing such fine clothes, with skin smooth, unblemished by wind, sun and spray, her hair fine and black, hanging in a perfect vertical.

*

They leave the harbour at dusk, as part of an ill-matched flotilla; some older and still under sail, while others, like theirs, fill the evening air with diesel fumes and the noise of progress. Cousin No. 1 takes the helm as the fleet moves towards open waters, while Lingwah, as he always does at this time of day, looks towards the shoreline and the jetties, thinking back. Sometimes doubting his memory, but always longing. It's been over ten years now, but not a day goes by that he doesn't remember. The skipper and Cousin No. 2 keep watch and look in particular towards the Chinese shore; they do this every time they sail these days. Mostly it is dark and quiet, but on occasion, they see Red Guards and Chinese patrol boats searching for people trying to swim across the narrow waters.

A few vessels follow them when they diverge from the main

route to the fishing grounds off Taipa, but one by one the others go their own way as they sail north, and by the time they are off Areia Preta, they are on their own. It is a calm night, an unremarkable October evening with the heat of the day just passed dissipated by a gentle breeze off the Pearl River. A few light clouds are illuminated by the half-moon, and the lights of the city and the Guia lighthouse are still clearly visible to port. They've been this way before many times, everybody has, but to Ling-wah, tonight feels different. He's never before been conscious of the moment that they cross into Chinese waters, after all there is no border line, no dotted line running over the surface of the sea, no border gate, but they all fall quiet as they continue north. Somehow, the atmosphere has changed. They all know that this time something is different. The skipper breaks the tension.

"Come on. Let's get started."

Cousin No.1 cuts the engine to an idle while the skipper and Cousin No.2 start to drop the purse seine, and Ling-wah prepares some long lines with an eye on the grouper that are supposed to be here, though he isn't optimistic; the tales about being able to hear them from the shore seem to be just that — tales. But their labour takes minds off unspoken worries. Three times they lower the net, tighten the seine line, and Cousin No.1 eases the boat forward; three times they raise the net full of sardines, snapper and bream. Even Ling-wah's long lines bring in a decent catch.

"Didn't I tell you? Let's get this sorted and get on our way back." The skipper is suitably smug, but even Cousins Nos. 1 and 2 are smiling and although they would never admit it, privately they have to concede that he was right to bring them here. The skipper laughs and slaps Ling-wah on the back.

Nets and lines are drawn in, the catch is stowed in ice-boxes, and Cousin No.1 turns the boat for home and goes to gun the engine. Nothing. He pulls the throttle lever back and tries again. Still nothing. The lever moves smoothly enough but the engine remains stubbornly in idle.

"Fuck!" Cousin No.1 swears remarkably rarely for a fisher-man, but this is one of those occasions. He pulls back on the throttle. "Something's wrong," he says.

"No shit," says the skipper. The good humour of only moments ago starts to disappear like a gambler's winnings. It is Cousin No.1's job to look after the engine – he is the only one thin enough to get into the crawl space beneath the deck. He cuts the engine, opens the access hatch, and curses as he squeezes through the narrow gap.

Two hours later and nothing has changed except their mood. Jubilation with their catch has moved through the stages of irritation and frustration with the engine, to growing anxiety. An increasing worry that is not helped when Ling-wah points out that they are drift-ing north, further into Chinese waters and closer to the Nine Islands themselves.

"Fuck," says the skipper. "You getting anywhere?" Cousin No.1 grunts something unintelligible from beneath deck and then sticks his head above the access hatch.

"The cable's good," he says. "It's the throttle valve that's stuck."

"Can you fix it?"

"What the fuck do you think I'm trying to do?"

None of the crew even notice the approaching patrol boat, so focused are they on the broken engine and the nearby rocks, until, that is, the first bullets ram into the side of the boat, tearing holes in the already fragile gunwales. Instinctively, they throw themselves flat on the deck, face down in the stink of the remains of their catch, before another round of gunfire smashes the wheelhouse windows.

"What the...? Shit! Can't you get that fucking engine going?"

He saw her often. Round quiet corners of disused jetties, standing on wharves as a freighter was unloaded. On fishing boats and ferries. Nobody he knew ever believed him when he tried to tell them about her. Parents, teachers, school friends. The kinder ones thought he was just making it all up, they said that he had an imagination for sure, but they soon got tired of him going on about her. Those who were less kind wondered whether he was right in the head and looked at him strangely. They opined that he needed a good beating to get this nonsense out of him. Either way, young though he was, he got the message and stopped talking about her. He certainly didn't tell them about the final time.

For once she was seated, not standing. She was alone on a sampan that was drawn up on the wharves of the Inner Harbour. The fishing fleet was in and she watched on as catches were taken ashore; it seemed to the boy that she must have been getting in the way, and he couldn't understand why nobody seemed to notice she was there. Everyone was oblivious to her, as they carried boxes of fish to women waiting with carts. She looked contented as the activity whirled around her. The boy stared at her and wondered why nobody else could see the woman in the bright red dress, and for the first time in their encounters she looked back at him. She smiled and although they were a distance apart, he could see her eyes, full of love and caring. He wanted nothing more than to be with her, but the moment they shared was broken when his view was interrupted by a thickset man pushing past him, swearing at him to get out of the way. When the man had gone, the woman was no longer there and the sampan was empty. Devastated, he looked around to see where she might be, but there was no sign of her anywhere.

The junk has started to take on water. The gunfire has stopped, at least they think it has, they haven't heard anything in a while, but nobody knows how long it has been, and none of them is in much of a rush to get up off the deck to see. Finally, the skipper tells Ling-wah to take a look – this is the privilege of being the youngest – and gingerly, Ling-wah raises himself so that he can just about see over to where they think the gunboat had been. He can't see a thing. The clear, moon-lit sky has been replaced by a dense fog that seems to have come from nowhere and which swallows up any sound. The sea is calm and still - he guesses that they are still drifting towards the rocks, but without being able to see it is impossible to tell for sure. Ling-wah whispers that everything seems to be okay and the others slowly clamber to their feet, looking about them anxiously, expecting a gunshot at any moment. The skipper surveys the damage to his boat without saying a word, but the pain is in his face. Cousin No. 2 grabs a bucket and starts bailing out. They are all silent, terrified that the gunboat is listening out for them.

He feels a deep warmth when he sees her. She is standing on the water, off the starboard side of the shattered fishing junk. Through the fog, her red dress glows like a beacon calling him towards her, summoning him. He knows what he has to do and isn't afraid; he's been waiting for this day for the last ten years. He knew it would come. Cousin No. 1 is back working on the engine, Cousin No. 2 is still bailing out, and the skipper is trying to repair some of the damage to the wheelhouse; none of them have a chance to stop him when he steps over the side and walks towards her, and by the time he hears their voices calling after him, he is lost to them in the fog. Ling-wah knows that she will look after them, and in the distance he hears the engine start.

All will be well; all will be as it should be.

River Crossing with Night Herons

The water is the colour of the *yuenyeung* coffee that starts my day, though when the algae blooms, the river resembles a carefully manicured lawn, as if one might simply walk across it.

If only.

Close to the city, barges and dredgers join together in a forest of floating cranes, while further out along the main channel, larger vessels head out to sea, and further out still...well, that's the other side.

But it's all so different now from how it once was; when two young lovers stepped gingerly into the water under a clouded, moon-less night.

They left their village in the quiet before dawn. The Red Guards had arrived two months earlier, and since then, each day had been marked by public denunciations. The schoolmaster had been first, forced to admit that he had been teaching George Eliot. The shopkeeper was accused of cheating his customers by leaning on the scales when he weighed out the rice. One farmer was blamed for the drought that had left half the fields barren, another for the flooding that had left the rest water-logged.

Theirs had been a secret love. Their families had been at odds for as long as anyone could remember, and for reasons no-one could recall, but the arrival of the Red Guards had made petty differences irrelevant. Of far more immediate concern to the boy and girl was the announcement that all young people in the village were to be sent away to unlearn their crimes. The two lovers would be separated. They would be apart for the first time in their lives.

I'm slow to get out of bed these mornings. The arthritis is

getting worse. I don't sleep much and when I lie awake in the night, I listen to my heart beating. It feels faint and uncertain, as if my body is unsure whether to continue, or whether perhaps it is time to rest for good. I am unconcerned by this and I have accepted that soon the day will come when I don't wake. Until then, I think of her and see her as she was; young and pretty, with a slender face and eyes that looked upon the world as something to explore. Sometimes, I think I see her in the street and when I do, she hasn't aged. Unlike me. When I look in the mirror, all I see are lines and liver spots.

They had been travelling for days, losing track of how long they had been on the move. First by bicycle and then on foot. Wherever possible they took unmarked paths, avoiding villages and towns. Avoiding people, avoiding detection. They scavenged for food or went hungry, and slept in fields or abandoned buildings, holding each other close to keep away the dark. The girl pushed away the unwanted thoughts that came to her unbidden when they stopped moving; the memory of the time nine weeks ago when she had become a young woman and he a young man. She wonders how she can tell him.

I live alone with no-one to look after me; no children to help me, no grandchildren for me to spoil. When I see my neighbours handing out the lai see packets at New Year, there is always a sense of what if? There will be nobody to leave offerings after I've gone, when my heart finally decides that one more beat is just not worth the effort. I worry that nobody will know, until the police have to break down the door and find a putrefying body, much like they did all those years ago.

Eventually they arrive at a place where they have to wade through streams and push their way through thickets of bamboo. Now they are standing in a mangrove swamp, at the water's edge, watching the lights beckoning from across the water.

It looks further than they expected and the girl is nervous, fiddling with a necklace that he gave her. She has never before swum further than the length of a small lake back home — barely more than a pond — where the village children would cool off from the summer heat.

"We'll never make it that far," she says.

"Of course we will, trust me. Anyway, we can't go back now." This is true. Even if they could make it back to the village, the punishment they would face would be worse than going forward. The boy takes her hand. She is shaking and he holds her tight. "But we won't get across dressed like this, our clothes will drag us down."

They strip to their underwear; she turns away, although there is nothing to see yet. Still they delay, thinking of families left behind, only the white-eared night herons breaking the silence. Finally, the boy speaks.

"Follow me." He puts one foot into the water. It is colder than he expected, and he can feel the mud and ooze between his toes. Slowly, he adjusts to the temperature, but he has to fight to resist the urge to turn back as he moves into the deeper waters and the strong, embracing current takes hold of him. Instead he goes on, goes towards the lights drawing him towards a different future.

"Come on," he says to the girl. "It's easy," he lies.

I come to this park when I can, aches and stiffness permitting. Today has been hot and although the sun is starting to set, the air is still charged with the heat of the day. I find myself struggling a little for breath, so I take a rest on a concrete bench where I can look across the water, think back and remember.

She joins me whenever I sit here and remember that night. Often, she shares the bench with me. Sometimes children play at our feet and she smiles at them indulgently as they run and jump, laugh and shout, and those are bittersweet times, when what might have been becomes hard to ignore.

It's not easy. The water is cold, the current strong. He kicks out from the bank but the river-grass catches around his feet. He stops to rest, his feet just reaching the river-bed, but the water laps against his mouth and he has to hold his lips tightly closed. He feels fish brushing against his legs. Or at least so he thinks; he has a fear of the unknown, the unseen, and he tries to put out of his mind the crabs, eels and shrimp that live beneath the surface. The boy looks back to the girl and can see that she is struggling. He should go back and help, but the lights beckon him forward.

To his surprise, it gets easier in the deeper water. He hears the girl behind him, but her strokes are erratic, desperate. She is floundering. He thinks she is saying something, but he can't make out what. Ahead, the lights are bright and now he can hear the sounds of life on the approaching shore. He has to choose between going forward, or back to help the girl. But he is tired himself, oh so tired. The cold has drained him of energy, his legs and arms are heavy and barely move in response to his commands.

The lights call out to him, urging him onwards.

I like to think I can see where we stepped out that night, but I know it's wishful thinking. There's been so much development since. Five gold stars on red flutter in the wind where egrets and cormorants once flew, and office blocks and apartment buildings stand in place of bamboo. At night, the other side of the river is illuminated by Samsung, Coca-Cola and Nike. The shoreline itself has moved. I wonder if things would have been different had the river been as narrow then as it is now. Perhaps then we would all have made it across.

He asks the police to look for her but it is three days before a fisherman finds her in the muddy waters beneath a pontoon. He can't bring himself to look at the body, already decaying and bloated, but he knows it's her from the necklace she wears. There is no need for an autopsy: she is just one of many, so she takes the truth with her and he will never know. When an appropriate time

The thing is, I'm actually the real deal. Not one of those fakes or tricksters who prey on people, the con artists who take advantage of them and make a few dollars out of their problems, keeping everybody happy by telling them what they want to hear. For the tourists, it's just one of those things they do when they come to Macau, along with eating, shopping and gambling. It's an act, a show; a game both sides play and everybody knows the rules. Me, I truly can see into the future, and believe me, I wish I couldn't. It's rarely anything to look forward to.

*

I have a client booked in for this morning. In the past, I worked the temples and the night-markets like the street-performers. I did *kau chim*, reading the sticks and interpreting the oracle, I was a master of face reading, palm reading – all the stuff I had to do to make a living. I went through the motions of what the punters expected of me, even though I could have answered their questions without any of that fakery. These days I'm an old man and I just do it my way; I don't care much for going out so I prefer to stay indoors. Luckily my reputation is such that I don't have to spend all day at the temple and instead they come to my apartment.

Today it's a young woman - a Miss Choi, no more than twenty - whose mother is ill. I can tell she's doubtful, wondering what she's doing in this somewhat tatty living room. She's attractive and smartly dressed in a modern style; jeans, a Versace T-shirt – or at least a Versace knock-off – and a gold necklace. Her looks only serve to emphasise the drab emptiness of the room. For the past few months, I've been slowly getting rid of things, divesting myself of a life. Little furniture remains, just enough for my needs. I ask her to take a seat on the worn, black leather sofa that continues to take up one side of the room. A framed photograph of my parents hangs on the wall.

I always like to let the client start, so I pull over a chair and wait for her to speak. When she does, her voice is quiet and hesitant and I can only just hear her over the sound of the ceiling fan gently stirring the air above us.

"I'm not sure why I'm here..." she starts, "I'm sorry, I don't mean to be rude but I don't believe in all this mumbo-jumbo." I don't take offence; the young ones are always like that. They pretend not to believe and yet still they come. The older generation believe implicitly without any apologies.

"There is no mumbo-jumbo, Miss Choi. I have certain skills, that is all."

And that's the truth of it: I've always had this ability, ever since I was a boy. I was seven when, out of the blue, I announced to my parents, "*Big Uncle's going to die.*" Big Uncle was my grandmother's brother. He lived alone on Coloane, down a dirt track, completely out of the way with no neighbours anywhere close and to my younger self, he seemed ancient, though in reality he must have been about the same age I am now. We had just left his home - my parents had wanted to ask him something - when the words came out. I must have shocked them; I certainly surprised myself. My father told me to be quiet and stop being so disrespectful of the elderly, but later my mother was more friendly, took me to one side and tried to explain how one day we would all die. "*No,*" I said, "*I mean he's going to die tomorrow.*" My mother drew back and slapped me hard across the face, sending me to bed with no supper.

The next day, Big Uncle died. A massive stroke that came out of the blue while he was playing mah-jong in the tea-shop.

Clients are always looking for hope, that's the worst of it, but because I know the truth, hope is the last thing I have to offer. Miss Choi wants to know that her mother will recover, that all will be well. But it won't and nothing I can say will alter this. Her mother will die shortly. All that is left is to try and tell her gently.

It will be a relief in some ways when all this is over.

*

When it comes down to it, people always ask about the same three things: health, business and love. I suppose these are the subjects that matter to us most. Will my mother get better? Should I invest in this stock? Will he make a good husband? I used to wonder why I only had bad news to give. Over time, I came to realise that people would mostly visit a fortune-teller because they had doubts — usually, well-founded ones. After all, why waste money if you know you're in love? Very occasionally, I was able to offer good news. More often than not, as today, an illness was incurable, a business investment unwise, or a lover unfaithful.

The grief everyone had felt over Big Uncle's death over-shadowed my prediction, which was somehow forgotten. Over the years, I've tried and failed to understand how it works, but when I was very young my skills were limited, crude. I could only see the most dramatic close events. As I got older, I was able to refine my abilities, to see things that were subtler and further away. To begin, it seemed a blessing - friends and family sought my opinion on everything and I was always popular at the dog track - but in time, it became relentless. It wasn't enough that I could see answers to specific questions; no, images of the future started to come to me unasked. I could be walking down the street and the destiny of strangers passing by would crowd in on me. I was being overwhelmed by the future, deafened by the fates of those around me.

Relationships became impossible. How could I love someone when I knew exactly what they were going to do or what was going to happen to them? When I was twenty, I went out with this girl for a while, but soon I knew she was seeing someone else. When I told her they were going to spend a weekend together in Hong Kong, she said that was nonsense. Two days later, she discovered that her new boy-friend had bought the ferry tickets. Girlfriends became suspicious of me, of my motives, of everything I said and did. They wondered what I knew and sometimes predictions became self-fulfilling.

The worst of it was when my parents died; my father went first, twenty years ago, and then my mother. Of course I knew, and they must have known that I knew, but it's the only time I've ever lied about the future. With my father, I had a general sense some months in advance which became stronger and more definite as the weeks progressed. When he fell ill, my mother asked me, *"Will he recover? You must know, so tell me, please."* I fudged my answer; I didn't want to lie but I couldn't tell the truth either. I said that I couldn't see clearly, I said that perhaps I was too close, that with family my vision was clouded. I doubt if my mother believed me and a year later, when she started having heart trouble, she asked me to be honest with her. She said she wanted to know so that she could put things in order if she had to.

Telling my mother she had only three months to live was the hardest thing I've ever had to do. That's when I retreated to my apartment here in Coloane, staying indoors away from people as much as I could. I've become something of a monk or a hermit and I think I now understand why Big Uncle lived here: it's as close as you can get in Macau to the middle of nowhere. I still need money to live on though, so I started taking private appointments.

*

Miss Choi tells me about her mother.

"The stomach pains started two years ago, I think. They may have started before that but my mother never said anything. I think she kept quiet about it, didn't want to worry my father."

"Tell me about them, your parents." I don't need to know, but she needs to tell me. Sometimes I'm part-therapist.

"They have a small restaurant on Taipa. It doesn't really make any money but it's my mother's passion. My father...he's not very practical...I don't know how he'll cope if anything happens to her..."

I have to decide whether to tell her that her father will die a few months after her mother. I often have this dilemma - they come to ask me about the future, but how much do they really want to know? Do they want the whole truth? I can't be dishonest: I will never lie to them, but I can decide how much to tell them. This time I elect against telling her unless she asks specifically. It's her mother she's come about not her father.

"My mother...?"

"I'm sorry, Miss Choi..." I don't need to say anything else. I think about taking her hand, but she draws herself inwards and I leave her to her thoughts for a time.

*

Miss Choi spends an hour with me in the end. I don't need all that time to tell her what she needs to know, but she needs the time to take it in. She's my final client and I'm in no rush, and anyway there's something about her that I respond to. We seem chalk and cheese, oil and water, but I'm drawn to her. Not in a sexual way – not at my age, and certainly not now – but I sense a connection. That's unusual. For all that I can see everything about a person's life, it is always very abstract; I feel no more about them than I do the weather. But with

Miss Choi it's different. I'm sorry for her of course, but more than that, there's something about her I can't see clearly and that intrigues me. Normally I can read people completely, but not with Miss Choi. There's a curtain I can't see beyond. I know what will happen to her parents, but nothing about herself. She blows her nose as she starts to gather her things. There have been a few tears, but I don't want her to go. That's another thing that is unusual: normally I'm anxious to be alone again.

"Would you like some tea before you go?" I ask. She looks at me, seemingly troubled by something beyond her mother, and accepts the offer. I go to the kitchen and when I return with a teapot and two cups, she is the one who takes my hand.

"Are you okay?" she asks. "Can I help? Is there anything I can do for you?"

I'm surprised by her questions. It's as if our roles have been reversed. Only slowly do I begin to understand.

"You know?" I ask.

"I'm sorry," she says.

"There's no need to be. I've known for a long time now. I'm prepared for it, it will be a blessing in some ways, but I wasn't prepared for this. For you knowing. You can see, can't you?"

"Yes."

She says this calmly, matter of fact and without much emotion. Perhaps that's a good sign for her future - she'll need to keep a sense of detachment.

When Big Uncle died, I was too young for it to register, but there were family stories about how he had second sight. When I was a young man, I came to understand that somehow his skills had passed to me upon his death - an inheritance of sorts, a transition between generations - and now they are passing to Miss Choi.

I will be dead tomorrow.

I've known for several months that my life was coming to an end, and more recently I've been able to foresee the time and date. Tomorrow afternoon, a little after lunch. When Big Uncle died, he didn't know that I was going to take up the burden, but I have a little time left still. Perhaps in the remaining hours, I can explain things to Miss Choi, tell her how it will be, offer words of advice. There was nobody to help me and there's so much that I need to tell her. Perhaps one day she'll also end up living in a small apartment on Coloane.

"Miss Choi, please, would you like to stay for dinner?"

A Photograph, Creased

I'm sure he's watching me when we're playing. I see him out of the corner of my eye, but when I look, he's reading his book. It's like a game, each of us trying to catch the other looking at them, but we never do. But still, I'm sure of it. Call it an old woman's intuition.

The four of us - myself, Mei-Mei, Siu-Lai and her cousin - are at our usual table at the back of the teashop. We spend most afternoons there playing mah-jong, gossiping, putting the world to rights. We talk about him while we play. He's been there for the last three days, just sitting with a pot of iron buddha. About my age, perhaps a little older. Mid-seventies say. Dressed in grey slacks and a plain, white polo shirt. He has a book with him. I think it's a guide to Macau, because I can see it has a picture of the ruins of St. Paul on the cover, but this isn't a tourist part of town. We shuffle the tiles and decide on one more hand before we call it a day.

Lei-Wai keeps an eye on the man when she's not serving her customers. You can tell that she doesn't know what to do about him. On the one hand, she's happy to take his money and why shouldn't he enjoy a cup of tea like anyone else? But on the other...well, I know she had family back in Nanjing, so I can imagine how she feels. He makes me feel uneasy. There's something in him that triggers memories that would be best left alone. He worries me. I don't tell the others this. They'd think I was crazy. Perhaps I am.

Siu-Lai draws a tile from the wall. It's the East Wind she's been waiting for and she wins again. I look towards where the man was sitting but he has gone. Somehow, I know that he will be back tomorrow.

The man is Japanese.

*

Yoshida Takamoto had been in Macau a week. Time was running out - his plane ticket told him that - but he was hesitating before going further. Back in Sapporo, it had all seemed so straightforward. There had been an inevitability about what he had done. A defined course of action that started with him hiring the private investigator and ended with an Air Macau A320 on its final approach.

He lay down on his hotel bed and thought about his father. Yoshida worried that he was betraying his memory. Would he approve of what he was doing? His father had never once mentioned Macau to him and Yoshida would expect better from his own son. But his father had saved the photograph, which he needn't have done. Had he wanted to, he could easily have destroyed it before he died. Instead, it was left with papers he must have known Yoshida would go through. What did he expect Yoshida to do?

Yoshida looked at the investigator's report again, as if this time it might have something new to tell him.

*

I visited the columbarium yesterday. It's six years since Mother died, but her ashes have not yet been moved. I burnt some offerings for her and then sat down in the shade on a concrete bench. I thought back to my childhood and those years just after the war. Mother told me my father died before I was born, so there was only the two of us. I sometimes dreamt that I had a brother and if I told Mother this, she would give me a funny look and tell me to stop talking nonsense. The dreams gradually became less frequent, until they stopped altogether.

Sometimes I wish I'd married, but mostly it doesn't bother me. There were boyfriends when I was younger, but whenever we started to get close they would drift away. They never said why, though there were rumours, they just moved on and things fizzled out. I used to cry, but Mother always said that it was for the best, which I never understood. Don't mothers always want their daughters to get married?

"What happened?" I would ask. "Why did they lose interest? Did you say something to them?"

Later I came to understand why and I was angry with her. There were tearful accusations and it was several years before we were reconciled.

*

Yoshida had spent his first few days in Macau getting his bearings. He did the tourist sights because he thought that he should, but although he wouldn't admit it, he knew he was avoiding the reason he came. By the fourth day, though, he decided that it was time to do something.

"Excuse me," he asked the young woman at the reception desk in his limited English. "Can you tell me how to get to here?" He showed her an address. The receptionist's English was only a little better than Yoshida's, but it was all they had in common.

"Why you want to go there?" she asked. "It no tourist place."

"I know. How do I go there?"

The receptionist consulted with a colleague before returning to Yoshida.

"You could take bus, but taxi better. I write address in Chinese for driver."

Yoshida knew that the receptionist was staring at him as he walked across the hotel lobby and out into the street.

After fifteen minutes of reckless driving, hard on the brakes, the taxi-driver deposited Yoshida in an unremarkable backstreet, in an unremarkable backwater of Macau. A narrow street, with six or seven-storey apartment blocks, all of which looked in need of repair. The concrete was stained, the metal-work rusting. The building he was looking for had once been painted a dark green. Now much of the paintwork had gone and what remained was flaking.

*

"Hongaan," said the stallholder under her breath as we left. I think I was about five or six. After the war anyway. I can still picture the scene. We were buying rice and vegetables in the market. I asked my mother what it meant, but she didn't answer. She had a shopping bag in one hand and dragged me along by the other. I could see she was crying. That was the earliest occasion I remember, but there were others.

Hongaan. Traitor.

There was the old man who lived nearby and spat at us if he saw us walking past. Women who would call out '*maaigwoktsaak*', which I didn't understand.

I hated school. The other children either ignored me or bullied me. They said my mother was a whore. I tried to become invisible, but the insults kept coming. The teachers were no better, and I was always being punished for breaking rules I didn't know existed. In the end I stopped going. It was easier that way.

'*Maaigwoktsaak*' Country-selling thief.

*

Yoshida stood at the entrance, looking at the doorbells for different apartments. He found the name but didn't press the button. Yoshida had no idea of what he would say, or even if she would be able to understand him. He spoke no Chinese and she wasn't likely to speak Japanese. He had to hope she might have a little English. Yoshida felt foolish just standing there, so he crossed the street to where there was a small sitting-out area.

He sat and watched the door, wondering if he would recognise her from the photograph that the investigator had given him. Somewhat to his surprise he did, and when an elderly woman, slightly stooped, wearing what looked like brown, paisley pyjamas, came out of the building, Yoshida followed her to a tea-shop. He took a table in a corner and watched her play mah-jong until he could drink no more tea.

*

When we are finished with mah-jong for the day, we gather the tiles and Mei-Mei puts her hand on mine. I've known Mei-Mei the longest. We worked at the same garment factory and spent forty years sewing shirts side by side until the factory closed down. She knew about my mother, but was never judgmental.

"It's you he's interested in," she tells me. She's right. I've known that from the first day. "Why don't you go and ask him what he wants?"

I know that would be the sensible thing to do, but why should I?

"If he has something to say to me, let him say it."

"Go talk to him," she says. I can tell that Mei-Mei wants to say something more, but doesn't like to.

Hesitantly, I walk over to where he's sitting. I can see that he's as nervous as I am unsettled. He puts down his tea, stands, and bows. A deep bow that does nothing to put me at ease.

"Who are you?" I ask. "Why have you been watching me?"

He answers in English, but I've no idea of what he's saying. I can sense his disappointment when he realises that I don't understand. He tries what I think is Japanese, but that's even worse. He gestures for me to sit and I do. I am no longer irritated by this man who has been watching me. Now I feel sorry that we can't talk. He says something in Japanese and for the first time I see that he has a small briefcase with him. He opens it and takes out a sheaf of papers that he places on the table. I'm nervous. The same feeling of unease I've had since the man first appeared, only worse as I wonder what the papers hold.

He searches through the documents until he finds what he's looking for: an old black-and-white photograph, creased from repeated folding. He pushes the photograph across the table towards me. A man and a woman are standing in the *Largo do Senado*. The man is holding a small boy by the hand; the woman is carrying a baby. The man is in military uniform. The woman is my mother. It shouldn't be a shock of course, but somehow it is. The photograph, faded as it is, makes it seem more real. I'd never seen a picture of him before. Mother had rarely wanted to talk about the war and if she had kept photographs, she never showed them to me.

And then there was the question of the little boy.

The others look on from a distance. The man is watching me. Judging my reaction. He tries again. I don't know enough English to understand what he's saying, but I do recognise one word as he points to the man in the photograph: Father.

He looks at me and says something else I don't understand.

Except for one word.

Brother.

The Price of Medicine

She remembered the first time. The two vodkas in the night-club had helped, but not much. When it was over she showered and scrubbed herself clean, but the scent of him lingered. The feel of his grasping hands. The hotel itself was bad enough; her mother would have been disgusted at the room. The carpet filthy, the paint peeling, stains on the sheets; she'd wondered how many times they'd been used since they were new. How many people had fucked in this same bed? It would kill her mother if she knew, which would be ironic.

Her mother.

Throughout the night she tried to ignore what was happening. She went through the motions the way she knew she must, the way Candy had taught her, and tried to imagine herself somewhere else. Tried to concentrate only on getting through being in a sordid ho-tel room with a strange man who had bad breath and smelt of cheap whisky. Thoughts of her mother kept returning, but she tried to banish them. She wanted to keep this separate; she didn't want to be remind-ed of soiled bed linen every time she saw her mother.

"You'll get used to it."

That's what Candy kept saying.

She wasn't sure whether that would be a good thing or not. Did she really want to get used to this? Did she want to accept it? For it to become normal? Better to keep it locked away – keep it apart; something she could cut out and throw away when it was over.

"Sometimes it's not so bad if you get a good-looking guy. Or a rich one. Give them what they want, tell them how good they are – any bullshit that makes them feel good – and they might give you extra. If they don't, just go through their wallets when they're having a piss."

Candy was from near Wuhan; her Putonghua rough and crude, a dialect Mei-Wa had difficulty following. Her own Putonghua was limited but she had to learn quickly; most of the punters in the club were mainlanders. Not the high-rollers - they went for the Russian girls - mostly just middle-ranking Party cadres, officials and business-men, who thought they were hot-shots but weren't. Mei-Wa had little in common with Candy, but was grateful for her friendship. The other girls had been wary, suspicious even; she was better educated than they were and they asked what she was after. It was Candy who had taken Mei-Wa under her wing, shown her the tricks of the trade. Taught her how to handle the men who were so drunk they couldn't get an erec-tion; taught her how to get punters to come as quickly as possible to get it over with and to move on to the next. More money that way.

More money. That was all that mattered.

The doctors were expensive and the medicines even more so.

*

"You're not our usual type," the owner had said. Mei-Wa had put out feelers to find somewhere. She got the address from a friend of a friend, who said she had a friend who knew someone who had worked there once. Mei-Wa turned up and asked to speak to the own-er. When she told him what she wanted, he took her into his office. She'd stood there like a cow for sale in a market while he looked her over. She fought to keep control when he felt her breasts; she wanted to hit him.

"Real. That's good. Have you done this before?"

"No."

"I didn't think so. Still, everyone has to start somewhere.

You're good-looking, I suppose. Nothing great, but good enough." He continued to appraise her. "But why? Why do you want to work here?"

"I need the money."

"Don't we all. But why here? Why not get some office job?"

"I need a lot of money. Quickly." She explained why. He looked doubtful.

"We're not a charity. If the girls are no good, I'll lose business." He thought for a moment. "Are you a virgin?"

"No." She remembered the supermarket manager and the fumbled awkward times in the store-room.

"Pity. A virgin can bring in really good money." He laughed. "It's fucking stupid, but it's the only job where you can get more for complete and total inexperience." He hesitated. "Okay, I'll give you a chance, but I'm warning you – any complaints and you're gone. What's your name?"

"Mei-Wa."

"No – your working name. You want something sexy, something Western. Something that sounds good to these mainland fuck-wits."

And so Tiffany was born.

*

Her mother was getting thinner. She had always been slight but her skin was becoming translucent; her hair thinning. She was dissolving in front of Mei-Wa's eyes. Sublimating. Soon she would be a ghost.

*

She had seen him before. In his fifties, overweight, balding; his hair combed over in a pretence so fake she had to make an effort not to laugh. He'd been in the club on a few nights, but had always gone with one of the others. Tonight, he beckoned her over and pulled close an empty chair. A bottle of brandy sat on the table and he poured two glasses, topping them up with Coke and adding ice. He asked her name and she told him Tiffany. He didn't tell her his.

Later, he is snoring. She's sore; he'd been rough. She wants to leave but he'd paid for the night and she remembers the owner's warning. His jacket is thrown over a chair. Quietly, she goes through the pockets and finds a wallet. There are US dollars, crisp and un-blemished notes, so many that she takes a fifty, knowing that it won't be missed, before putting the wallet back. In another pocket, there's a thin leather-bound pass which she opens and reads with alarm. She hears him turn over in bed and hurries back before she is missed.

*

Her father was lost and no longer knew what to do. He would spend his days drifting aimlessly, neglecting the antique shop which was her mother's love. Mei-Wa wanted to be angry with him, but knew that she couldn't. She knew that his life was falling apart and he was helpless to do anything about it. He wanted her mother to see a herbalist; inside Mei-Wa was screaming: *"What fucking good are a hand-ful of dried roots going to do when the cancer is eating her body?"* She wanted her mother to see a private consultant; the public hospital could only do so much. When her father objected that they didn't have the money, he didn't even ask how when Mei-Wa told him that she would look after it.

*

The man is there again the next night. He sees her and calls her over. She looks around for one of the other girls to go with her, but they are all occupied with clients. She has no choice and makes her way to his table.

"Last night was good, eh?" he leers. "I told you – I'm a fucking stud."

His hand is already on her thigh. She wants to take the knife that he'd been using to peel fruit and thrust it into his groin. She remembers who he is and says nothing.

"You're a Macau girl, right? I can tell. You Macau women are always better than Chinese girls. More sophisticated. I mean, look at them," he gestures in the direction of the room, "most of them would fuck a pig given the chance."

"What do you do?" She knows, of course, but wonders what he would say.

"Why do you care?"

The same hotel. The same treatment. The same pain.

*

The consultant looked at the test results. The X-rays and the scans. Mei-Wa stared out of the window. The consulting room overlooked a school playground and she watched children playing basketball. She could not read the expression on the consultant's face as his eyes looked from her to her mother. But her mother could and she took Mei-Wa's hand.

"It's okay Mei-Wa. It's okay."

Except that it wasn't.

*

He says he'll be in Macau for a week and wants her for the whole time. He pays the extra – but she needs more. She flatters him, polishes his ego to a shine. Does whatever it takes to get him to part with more of those crisp fifty and hundred dollar bills. She accepts all his demands, goes along with whatever degradation is necessary to pay for the intravenous doses of Adriamycin and Taxotere. Her mother now weighs less than ninety pounds. Mei-Wa can almost imagine carrying her mother, the way her mother must once have carried her. The nurses try not to catch her eyes. The doctors say there is nothing more they can do and talk of palliative care. There is a home they suggest. More expense.

*

She is sleeping – a shallow sleep from too much alcohol - when there is a rap on the door. A second knock and she rises to find out what somebody wants, but he is also awake and stops her. He grabs hold of her arms.

"Quiet!" he whispers. He pushes Mei-Wa into the bathroom. "Stay here," he says, as he closes the door. Suddenly she is wide awake, alert, terrified, wondering what the hell is going on. She hears the door being forced and then voices. Putonghua - guttural and angry, reminding her of Candy. There's an argument, that much is clear; she tries to make out the words but can't get enough of them. Suddenly a sharp crack sounds, then nothing.

The silence continues but she doesn't dare move as she sits on the cold floor. She stares at the pattern on the bathroom tiles; green and yellow flowers intertwined. She sees there is mould in the shower; the mirror is speckled with age. Eventually – she has no sense of time – she knows that she has to move. Slowly, not knowing what to expect or who may be on the other side, she turns the handle and opens the door an inch. When the door has cleared the frame, she looks through the narrow gap. Nothing. Except that now she can hear the sound of something dripping. Opening the door a fraction further, ever so slightly, she can see more of the room; a naked body – his naked body – lies on the bed, unnaturally still, head thrown back. She takes a deep breath, trying to quieten her heart. Cautiously, she opens the door completely, and slowly, step by step, she goes back into the bedroom. She cannot look, but she can't not look either. Her eyes are drawn to the body that she doesn't want to see; a body that she hates, but one with which she has become painfully familiar. A red stain has spread over the sheets and a line of blood is trickling to the edge of the bed. It falls into an ice bucket, which just a few hours earlier had held champagne.

His jacket is still where he left it, together with his wallet. She empties the wallet and leaves the room.

*

Her mother has died. Mei-Wa was crossing the road when it happened; she knew with such certainty that she bent double as a sharp pain ripped through her. While she recovered her composure, Mei-Wa sat on a concrete bench overlooking a small park and watched as a dog chased a pigeon. When she was ready, Mei-Wa called the hospice.

She had bought a double-niche in the columbarium on Taipa;

white marble pillars, beautiful and peaceful. There is a memorial garden shaded by willow trees, with a carp-filled pond and benches where families can sit and remember. When the ashes had been interred, Mei-Wa took her father's arm and led him down the hill to a taxi rank.

She wondered when would be the best time to tell him that she was pregnant.

The Jade Monkey Laughs

She's not sure which is her favourite. Sometimes it's the monkey. The face carved with such detail that she imagines the animal is watching her as she cleans the room. Making sure that she dusts thoroughly. That she doesn't miss anything. Other times it's the rooster, which is her sign. He has an erect tail with beautifully detailed feathers. This is not some humble farmyard bird; this is a proud creature confident of its place in the world. She can almost hear it crow. An authoritative call making sure that everyone knows who's in charge.

They sit in a glass cabinet in the lawyer's study. Twelve jade animals corresponding to the zodiac. They've been there longer than she has worked for Senhor Almeida and that's a long time. So long that she has to sit down for a moment to stop and work it out. She's seventy-three this year so that makes it…what, fifty-five? No, fifty-six years since she left Lam Fung's house and came to work for the Almeida family, one of Macau's oldest. Fifty-six years. She wonders where the time has gone. She would have had grandchildren by now, great-grandchildren even, if things had worked out differently. Fifty-six years soon to come to an end. It was ten years before she was even allowed in this room. She was only a kitchen maid then and it wasn't until the housekeeper died that she started coming into this inner sanctum. Even then she didn't have a key to the cabinet.

She had to steal that.

Six o'clock and the front door opens. Senhor Almeida comes home from his chambers at exactly the same time every day. It doesn't matter if it's summer, when the oppressive air is full and heavy, or whether the gutters and drains fill and threaten to overwhelm the streets. At six o'clock, she is standing by the door waiting for him. She takes his briefcase from the young assistant who helps him home these days, and – if he is carrying one – his umbrella. Sometimes she takes Senhor Almeida's arm and guides him into the entrance hall. *Good evening, sir* – she will say and he will reply in kind. He will not ask about her day. He no longer asks about her day the way he once did. When things were different. She will bring his dinner at seven and then, after he has eaten, Senhor Almeida will retire to his study and she will not see him again until morning.

The snake was the first one that she stole - carved from a jade disc so that it coiled in on itself. She didn't mean to steal it - that's what she tells herself - not at first anyway. She was just curious. It seemed harmless when she took the key from the desk and removed the delicate jade carving from the cabinet. She turned the snake over in her hand, admiring the intricate craftsmanship. She wondered how old it was? That was all she wanted to know when she took it to the antiques dealer on the Rua de Santo Antonio.

"Where did you get this from?" the dealer asked when he had finished examining the snake with his eyeglass.

"From my mother." She didn't know why she lied.

The dealer moved to the door and turned a sign from open to closed.

"It's lucky you came to me and not to somebody less honest. Do you have any idea of how old this is?"

"No."

"This is late Ming. Four hundred years old. Give or take a few decades."

She was silent as she took this in. There was of course another question that she had to ask. He answered before she spoke.

"You want to know what this is worth? I couldn't say, I could only guess, but collectors would pay a lot."

Later, with the snake safely returned to its place in the cabinet, she looked at the jade animals with renewed interest.

*

She had taken it calmly when he told her that he would be leaving Macau. Thinking about it later, she was not sure if she believed him. He had been born in Macau and they had been together for so long.

"I'm going to Portugal to live with my niece."

Yes, his eyesight was failing, but did he not trust her to look after him? There was a time when she would have trusted him with anything. How long ago was that? She can no longer remember, but she does remember his touch. His hand on her cheek. His lips.

She thought nothing more about the snake until the day she saw a piece of jade in a market meant for tourists. You didn't need to be an expert to know that it wasn't real jade – just a cheap jade-like stone – but the snake design was the same. Not as beautifully worked of course, nothing like the detail and quality, but still, at first glance, if you didn't look too closely…

She bought the snake.

They were going to be married, she and Senhor Almeida. His family had been doubtful, a lawyer and a housekeeper, but he had won them round until someone started spreading rumours. Lam Fung's wife she assumed, but didn't know for sure. She got the blame for the whole thing, as if Lam Fung had had nothing to do with it. As if he hadn't forced himself on her in the kitchen that night. She never got the chance to tell her side of the story.

She started visiting the markets and bric-a-brac shops looking for other cheap jade pieces. They had to be of a reasonable quality and they had to look like Senhor Almeida's collection. They were hard to find, but gradually, over the weeks and months, she added to the snake. A bull standing proudly. A dragon with scales along its back and tail, mouth open ready to breathe fire. Rat, sheep, horse, rooster, dog, pig, rabbit and finally a tiger; one by one, she replaced the precious Ming in the display cabinet with their imitations. All except for the monkey. As hard as she tried, she could never find a monkey that quite matched the original.

If it hadn't been for the abortion, perhaps she could still have won Senhor Almeida round. She never found out who told him. Even Lam Fung's wife didn't know about that. Lam Fung had paid for it and given her money to disappear for a time. Not that it mattered how Senhor Almeida knew. It was enough that he did.

*

"Suppose I had an almost full collection?" she asked the antiques dealer. "Would you be interested?"

"All twelve?"

"Eleven. Not the monkey."

"I'd need to see them, but yes, I'd be interested."

"How much?"

The dealer gave her a number that was more than she had expected. More than enough to give her a very comfortable life once Senhor Almeida had left. Surely she deserved something after all this time? After the broken promises?

As the weeks to the lawyer's departure grew closer, she supervised the packing of his life. The things that were to be sold; that were to go to charity; that were to go to Portugal. With the house in chaos, Senhor Almeida retreated more and more into his office, which was where she found him one morning.

"Senhor…," she was momentarily caught off-guard finding the lawyer sitting at his desk. "I didn't know you were here. I'll come back later." She started to leave the room.

"Wait," he called after her. "There's no need to go. Stay. Come, sit down and take a moment." She sat on an uncomfortable rosewood chair that she had never liked and noticed with apprehension that he was holding the dragon. She tried not to watch as he turned it round and round in his fingers. Could he tell that it was a fake? An interloper?

"How are you today, Senhor?" She tried to keep her voice calm. "I think the packing is going smoothly."

He ignored her polite inquiry. "In my mind's eye, I can still see every detail of this dragon. These days, I can barely make out its shape, but I can remember the intricacy of the scales. The nostrils flaring. The sharp arrowhead of the tail. Now…well, I can just about see that it's a dragon and not a rat." He changed the subject: "How long have you been with me?"

"It's been fifty-six years, Senhor."

"Fifty-six eh? That long? Longer than most marriages." She winced inwardly and wondered if he had said that deliberately. "I've been remiss," he continued, "too caught up in myself and my own future to ask about you. What are your plans after I've gone?"

"I'll stay with a friend for a time until I can find somewhere to live. Then, well…we'll see. What will be…"

"I should have done something for you. Fifty-six years, you should have some reward for putting up with me for so long. This dragon and its companions – they must be worth something. You could sell them; they'd give you some money to live on after I've gone."

"Senhor, that's too kind, I don't know what to say." In truth, she really did not know what to say. Did he know? Was this some kind of joke?

"Jade has a very special feel to it. Cold, hard, tough even, and yet smooth at the same time. But, do you know, after a while it starts to feel warm in the hand, almost alive." She watched as he ran his fingers over the dragon's back. "Perhaps though, I should take one of them to Portugal with me as a keepsake. The monkey, I think. Would you get it for me?"

She stood and took the monkey from the cabinet and placed it on the desk in front of him. He held it in his hands.

"It's true what they say about losing your sight. The way your other senses compensate. Even though I'm not yet fully blind, my hearing is sharper than it was, almost as though I was a young man again. And my sense of touch…it is remarkable you know…I think I could tell the difference between two feathers. I could tell a green olive from a black by feel alone." He stopped caressing the jade figures and looked at her. In spite of his approaching blindness, she felt as if he could see into her soul.

"I'm…" She started to speak but he stopped her with a raised hand.

"Please leave now. I'd like to be alone for a while."

As she left the room and closed the door behind her she was convinced that she could hear the monkey laughing.

From Somewhere the Scent of Jasmine

In the confused half-light of dawn, his wife is talking about her ancestral village, a few miles from Suzhou. She describes the house that her grandparents owned before the local Party took it; a house they'd had to abandon when the family fled from Shanghai to Macau when she was five. He turns to ask her if she can really remember it in such detail when she was so young at the time, but the bed is empty, and he realises that he has been dreaming of her again.

The pain usually comes in the middle of the night. Wei Chan wakes with the feeling that something is crawling up his throat and then he starts to cough and retch, longing but failing to throw up as the burning spreads its tendrils across his chest. He blames something he ate *("It's that Szechuan food, it'll be the death of me one day")*; his shop *("The landlord wants to increase the rent")*; his neighbours *("Karaoke all night")*. When the attack has passed, he lies in bed perspiring, trying to get back to sleep. This is when his wife comes to him.

*

His shop was one of several on the *Rua de Santo Antonio.* On weekdays, he didn't open until the afternoon; nobody bought antiques in the morning, so if necessary, he had time to recover from a disturbed night. Congee for breakfast always seemed to help. When his strength permitted, he would rearrange the stock that wasn't moving. On Mondays, he went over the accounts and the previous week's sales, a task that was taking him less time these days. On some mornings, his daughter Mei-Wa would visit, bringing with her his new grandson.

"When are you going to get this door fixed?" she asked, after fighting with it. The door was warped and would stick shut whenever it rained.

"I know, I know, it's on my list. Here, let me take him." Wei Chan held the baby, while his daughter struggled to close the door behind her. "How's our little Emperor, eh? How's little Bi-Bi?" He tickled Bi-Bi under the chin until a smile appeared, soon to be followed by cries.

"He was sleeping before, now look what you've done." She took back her son and held him with one arm, while removing a pile of newspapers from a chair. "This place is a mess. It's no wonder you never have any customers. Have you seen the new shop at the far end of the *Travessa*? It's got marble floors, automatic sliding doors. Beautiful orchids everywhere. Really smart." He knew the place she meant. It was obvious to anyone that it was doing well. What only skilled eyes could see was that most of the stuff it sold was fake. Fresh from the antique factories in Zhuhai and Shenzhen.

"Anyway, how are you doing today?" Mei-Wa asked, her eyes glued to her phone. He hadn't wanted to tell her about the pain at first - after all, it was just a little indigestion - until one morning she had found him bent double.

"Same as usual. OK, really."

"Well, you know what I think." Wei Chan didn't reply and he knew that she wasn't expecting an answer. She'd been going on at him to give up the shop and move in with her. Perhaps it would make sense, but he wasn't ready for that, and anyway he half-suspected that all she really wanted was a live-in babysitter.

"How long do you expect to be?" he asked. Mei-Wa had taken to leaving the baby with him when she was working. Not that he knew what she did, just that it was something that involved meetings at irregular hours and long phone calls. When working, she called herself Tiffany. She wore their jewellery. He hated having to call her Tiffany and avoided doing so whenever he could, but she had chosen the name herself. To him, she would always be Mei-Wa.

"Two hours or so. Maybe three. I'll be back before you open."

*

His three porcelain Tang *sancai* horses are probably the best things on display. But neighbouring shops have better examples and two of them have a little damage. The third is the one that he is particularly fond of. It's better quality than the others and while the rest have the horse standing on all four feet, in this one the right front leg is raised, ready to step forward. His wife had taught him what to look for: the quality of the glaze, the colour, fine details. He takes care when he dusts them, as he does every week.

His grandson is not difficult to look after. He's made up a cot for him and his daughter always leaves a few toys. Wei Chan once hoped to leave the business to her when he stopped, but she had laughed when he suggested it. *"Why would I want this load of old crap?"* had been her reply. He knows she doesn't really mean it and that the words come from her own pain. Perhaps his grandson might have taken over the shop, but Wei Chan is too old to keep the shop going that long.

It's a good day for business. One of the best for a while. Three tourists come in and one them buys a small plate decorated with a delicately painted pavilion. Between customers, he prepares his medicine. Apparently, there is disharmony between his stomach and liver, and the doctor has given him a mixture of pinellia, licorice root, white peony root and fresh ginger to infuse in water. He says that this will restore balance.

*

The pain is more frequent now. It has started to come most nights and Wei Chan is subtly attuned to its characteristics, like an old friend. He can tell how severe the attack will be and how long it will last by how far the pain spreads in the first few minutes. Last night was particularly bad and he slept only fitfully after it had passed. Even though it is only a dream, it is a comfort to him when he sees his wife. This time she was standing in the bedroom, dressed in her red cheong-sam, as she had been thirty-five years ago on their wedding day. As in life, she didn't hesitate to let him know what she thought, telling him not to be too hard on Mei-Wa who had done more than he could possibly know to help. Telling him not to spoil Bi-Bi. That his wife never saw their grandson hurts him almost as much as the pain that comes in the night.

"You look worse than usual," Mei-Wa said the next morning. "Really pale."

"Just a bad night. I'm fine."

"Have you been to the doctor? A real one I mean, not that quack." His daughter wanted him to see a Western doctor, but he prefers the old ways. The hospital had done nothing to help his wife.

"Let's not argue. How's little Bi-Bi?"

"Still not sleeping through the night."

"That makes two of us then."

While Mei-Wa leaves as Tiffany, and does whatever it is that she does, Wei Chan takes one of the horses and shows it to his grandson. His eyes light up and stubby hands reach out to touch it. Wei Chan lets him feel the horse, while taking care to keep a safe hold. The boy's hands explore the head and then he runs his fingers down the mane. The boy takes after his grandmother, Wei Chan thinks.

That night is pain-free for once, but his wife still comes to him. They are standing in front of a beautiful courtyard house built in a classical style and guarded by stone lions. Wooden doors carved with images of carp. Green-glazed dragons keeping watch from the roof-ridge. Through the main entrance, Wei Chan can see into the first courtyard. A lily pond surrounded by rose bushes and kumquat trees. From somewhere, there is the scent of jasmine. It is the middle of the day, but he knows that it will be cool and peaceful in the house. His wife smiles at him and says, *"Shall we go inside?"* She walks through the doorway, but he can't move. She turns and looks at him: *"It's beautiful in here. Come and join me."* He wants to follow her, to walk hand in hand through the courtyard, but he can't and he stays rooted to the spot while she disappears into the house.

*

"Do you ever think about your mother?'

"What?" Mei-Wa had been feeding Bi-Bi and was wiping his mouth with a tissue. "Of course I do. Why do you say that?"

"You didn't come with me last Ching Ming." It had been a cause of friction between them that Mei-Wa hadn't joined him in leaving offerings.

"What are you saying? You think I don't care? I had business to see to, I told you that."

"This shop was her idea," Wei Chan continued. "She had such an eye for antiques." He ran his finger over the counter, leaving a line in the dust.

"Tell me something I don't know. I know the shop was her love. Her favourite child. She made that clear often enough." As if regretting her bitter tone, Mei-Wa softened: "Let me cook for you tonight," she said, her hand on her father's arm. "I'll come round and make your favourite hotpot. It will do you good; I don't think you're eating properly."

When his daughter had left, Wei Chan sat his grandson on his lap and opened an old photograph album. "See there? That's your grandmother when she was young. Wasn't she beautiful? And here's one when your mother was the age you are now." Bi-Bi played with the pages of the album and made a series of noises that Wei Chan longed to imagine were words but weren't.

Later in the morning, when the pain comes, he is caught by surprise. It had rarely come during the day. He knows at once that it is different this time. There is a quality to it that he hadn't experienced before, as it subsumes his whole body. Rivers of pain running from a never-ending source somewhere deep in his chest, his breath short and difficult. But there is one thing that he must do, so he grips the arms of the chair he was sitting in and forces himself to stand up. When he does, the door opens and his wife enters. She is wearing the same skirt and blouse that she had on the day they opened the shop. *"There you are,"* she says, standing on tiptoes and kissing him on the cheek. He can smell her perfume; feel the touch of her lips. *"Come on, we'll be late."* Taking him by the hand, she leads him out of the door and rather than being in the *Rua de Santo Antonio,* they are standing in front of the courtyard house. *"Are you ready this time?"* she asks. He cannot speak, his breathing is laboured and the pain is wrapping itself around his body like a snake, but he manages to nod and they pass through the doorway into the cool, jasmine-scented courtyard.

*

When Mei-Wa returns, her arms burdened with shopping bags of lotus root, bak choi and pork, she is puzzled to find the shop empty. She calls out repeatedly, increasingly worried. There is no sign of her father, but she finds Bi-Bi sitting contentedly in his cot, smiling and playing with a Tang horse. Mei-Wa picks up her son and holds him close while she searches the shop. She sees her mother everywhere. In the hand-painted ginger jars and the blue and white glazed bowls; in the *wucai* rose vase and the gold-threaded Guan pieces. It had been too painful for her to go to the columbarium with her father at Ching Ming but she'd regretted not going ever since. She looks into Bi-Bi's eyes which seem to be speaking to her, telling her that it will be alright. *We're together*, he says.

Author Biography

In 2014 Graeme Hall abandoned the world of intellectual property law to become a novelist and short story writer. He has won the short story competitions of the Macau Literary Festival and the Ilkley Literature Festival, and his writing has been published in anthologies by Black Pear Press and the Macau Literary Festival.

Graeme lived in Hong Kong from 1993 to 2010 and still keeps a close connection to the city. His first novel was set in Hong Kong and Shanghai over the period 1996/97 and most of his writing comes from his love of that part of the world. Graeme first visited Macau in 1993 and he quickly became fascinated by the oldest European settlement in Asia. That visit was just the first of many trips to explore Macau's unique mixture of Europe and China, and also to enjoy the *chorizo* and *vinho verde*. His current work in progress is a novel set in Macau in the years immediately following the Second World War.

He is an active member of the Leeds Writers Circle whose members have been a constant source of advice, support and encouragement.

Graeme lives in Calderdale, West Yorkshire with his wife and a wooden dog.

About Fly on the Wall Press

A publisher with a conscience.
Publishing high quality anthologies on pressing issues,
chapbooks and poetry products, from exceptional poets around the
globe. Founded in 2018 by founding editor, Isabelle Kenyon.

Other publications:
Please Hear What I'm Not Saying
(February 2018. Anthology, profits to Mind.)
Persona Non Grata
(October 2018. Anthology, profits to Shelter and Crisis Aid UK.)
Bad Mommy / Stay Mommy by Elisabeth Horan
The Woman With An Owl Tattoo by Anne Walsh Donnelly
the sea refuses no river by Bethany Rivers
White Light White Peak by Simon Corble
Second Life by Karl Tearney
The Dogs of Humanity by Colin Dardis
Small Press Publishing: The Dos and Don'ts by Isabelle Kenyon
Alcoholic Betty by Elisabeth Horan
Awakening by Sam Love
Grenade Genie by Tom McColl
House of Weeds by Amy Kean and Jack Wallington
No Home In This World by Kevin Crowe

Social Media:
@fly_press (Twitter)
@flyonthewall_poetry (Instagram)
@flyonthewallpoetry (Facebook)
www.flyonthewallpoetry.co.uk

More from Fly on the Wall Press...

Alcoholic Betty by Elisabeth Horan

ISBN10 1913211037
ISBN13 9781913211035

The brave and vulnerable poetry collection of Elisabeth Horan's past relationship with alcohol. Unflinchingly honest, Horan holds a light for those who feel they will not reach the other side of addiction.

"This is the hole. I go there
On Sundays. I go there after dinners
Before school --- mid work day
After lunch with the boss Mondays

The hole has Hangover coal
To paint my face to smudge
In the acne, rosacea, colloscum"

"Alcoholic Betty, we know the story. She died. Or did she? Through the "hours of penance" that is alcoholism and its attendant chaos-math and aftermaths, recurrent false dawns and falsetto damnations, Elisabeth Horan forges a descent/ascension pendulum of fire poems that are not "a map to martyrdom" - but a call to "go nuclear - Repose. Repose." Alcoholic Betty, we know the story. She died. She died so she could live."

- Miggy Angel, Poet, Author and Performer